THE RIGHT TO **READ** PLANTS A SEED

ORANGE YOU GLAD TO READ LIME?

I'M FOR LIME

SAVE THE LIME BOOKS!

PRINT *THIS* TINT

NO ONE WINS WHEN A BAN BEGINS

DOWN WITH LIME BOOKS!

by Jan Zauzmer

illustrated by Blanca Millán

In loving memory of Ezra
—J. Z.

Copyright © 2025 by Jan Zauzmer
Illustration copyright © 2025 by Blanca Millán
All rights reserved.

Published by Familius LLC, www.familius.com
PO Box 1130, Sanger, CA 93657

Familius books are available at special discounts for bulk purchases, whether for sales promotions or for family or corporate use. For more information, contact Familius Sales at orders@familius.com.

Reproduction of this book in any manner, in whole or in part, without written permission of the publisher is prohibited.

Library of Congress Control Number: 2025935871

Print ISBN 9781641703994
Ebook ISBN 9798893960815

Printed in China

Edited by Michele Robbins and Leah Welker
Cover and book design by Brooke Jorden

10 9 8 7 6 5 4 3 2 1

First Edition

Paige and her pals picked out teal books
and red books and plum books and more—
so many they spilled from the shelves to the floor.

The more the kids piled,
the more the kids smiled.

But not everyone thought that this rainbow was grand—
some wanted lime-colored books to be banned.

None had more zest
for this lime-bashing quest . . .

than a bigwig in town named Ms. Vicky,
who dreamed up a scheme that was icky:
"Let's meet at the neighborhood hub
to start a new Down with Lime Club."

Huge numbers turned out
to hear Vicky spout.

They were all ears
as she whipped up their fears:
"Who can relax
with lime in the stacks?"

"Not us!" called the throng.
"Lime is plain wrong."

Then she rattled the room
with this picture of doom:
"If we don't remove lime,
we could end up with slime!"

So the gang made a plan to launch a lime ban.

On one eerie and dreary and uncheery night,
they scoured the library left and then right
and sneakily snatched every lime book from sight.

The very next morning,
without any warning,
not a trace of bright green
was there to be seen.

"Where did the lime books go?"
Paige's class wondered.

"Wouldn't you like to know!"
Vicky's crew thundered.

News of the missing books speedily spread faster than butter on freshly baked bread.

Not long after dawn,
folks flocked to the lawn.
With the town in a tizzy,
reporters got busy.

Next to appear . . .
Vicky—oh dear!

"Lime books should not be allowed!"
she cried to the crowd.

"But why?" asked the team of school leaders.
"Why peel the lime books away from our readers?"

"Because lime is weird,"
Vicky sneered.

Mayor Brooks soon proposed a smart fix:
"Give families a mix of these colorful picks
so that they get to choose
from books of all hues."

Not the slightest bit shy,
Vicky roared in reply:
"My club left you orange, tan, even hot pink.
This plan of ours helps us control what you think.
Purple and peach and maroon are okay.
So are lavender, yellow, and elephant gray.
But lime is just not who we are.
That color goes one shade too far."

Together the teachers yelled out from the bleachers: "From Vail to Vermont, here's what we want: all kinds of pages at all the right ages."

Librarian Reid
completely agreed:
"From pre-Ks to twelves,
let's fill empty shelves.
With so much to learn,
let's give lime books a turn."

The grown-ups were stuck in a clash
'til one kid made a mighty big splash.

"Hey, I have something to say!"

hollered Paige from the stage.
"There's no reason or rhyme
to get rid of lime.
To each bandit who banned it:
We kids won't stand it!"

So Paige in the front led her pals on a hunt. They searched crannies and nooks to find hidden books.

This was far and away
the best library day!

Jotting down notes,
the reporters got quotes.
"How do you track down a book?"
"It's simple—we look!"

"You kids should be proud,"
said the mayor aloud
as she waved a decree
for the heroes to see.
"I have news that is splendid:
The lime ban has ended!"

TO THE KIDS WHO SAVED THE BOOKS:
THANKS FROM MAYOR BROOKS

Then the children raced home to read copies with their parents and nanas and poppies.

On a whim and a hunch, they'd grabbed a whole bunch,

every copy they could—

those lime books sure must be good!

LIME DRIVES US BANANAS

BOO THIS HUE

DOWN WITH LIME BOOKS!

LIME'S TOO TART

LIME GREEN IS NOT OUR SCENE

HIGH TIME TO SQUEEZE OUT LIME